A LOOK AT US HISTORY

THE SPANISH-AMERICAN WAR

BY MARIE ROESSER

Gareth Stevens PUBLISHING

Please visit our website, www.garethstevens.com. For a free color catalog of all our high-quality books, call toll free 1-800-542-2595 or fax 1-877-542-2596.

Cataloging-in-Publication Data

Names: Roesser, Marie.
Title: The Spanish-American War / Marie Roesser.
Description: New York : Gareth Stevens Publishing, 2020. | Series: A look at U.S. history | Includes a glossary and index.
Identifiers: ISBN 9781538248836 (pbk.) | ISBN 9781538248850 (library bound) | ISBN 9781538248843 (6 pack)
Subjects: LCSH: Spanish-American War, 1898--Juvenile literature.
Classification: LCC E715.R64 2020 | DDC 973.8'9--dc23

First Edition

Published in 2020 by
Gareth Stevens Publishing
111 East 14th Street, Suite 349
New York, NY 10003

Editor: Therese M. Shea

Photo credits: Series art Christophe BOISSON/Shutterstock.com; (feather quill) Galushko Sergey/Shutterstock.com; (parchment) mollicart-design/Shutterstock.com; cover, p. 1 DE AGOSTINI PICTURE LIBRARY/De Agostini/Getty Images; p. 5 dikobraziy/Shutterstock.com; p. 7 Historical/Corbis Historical/Getty Images; pp. 9, 11, 17, 19, 21, 29 Everett Historical/Shutterstock.com; p. 13 The Frent Collection/Corbis Historical/Getty Images; p. 15 Photo 12/Universal Images Group /Getty Images; p. 23 Time Life Pictures/ The LIFE Picture Collection/Getty Images; p. 25 https://commons.wikimedia.org/wiki/File:John_Hay_signs_Treaty_of_Paris,_1899.JPG; p. 27 https://commons.wikimedia.org/wiki/File:Battle_of_Paceo.jpg.

Printed in the United States of America

CPSIA compliance information: Batch #CW20GS: For further information contact Gareth Stevens, New York, New York at 1-800-542-2595.

CONTENTS

Words in the glossary appear in **bold** type the first time they are used in the text.

AMERICA AT WAR

In 1898, the United States fought a war against Spain. One of the reasons for the war was to help Cubans win **independence**. After the war, the United States gained **territory** in Latin America and in the western Pacific Ocean.

MAKE THE GRADE

Latin America is an area made up of Mexico, Central America, South America, and some islands in the Caribbean Sea.

LATIN AMERICA

FIGHTING FOR FREEDOM

In February 1895, the people of Cuba began to fight for their country's independence. At that time, Cuba was a **colony** of Spain. Spanish leaders forced Cuban **rebels** into camps called *reconcentrados*. Thousands died from illness and hunger in these camps.

MAKE THE GRADE

US newspapers showed Cubans suffering in the camps. Americans wanted to help the Cuban rebels.

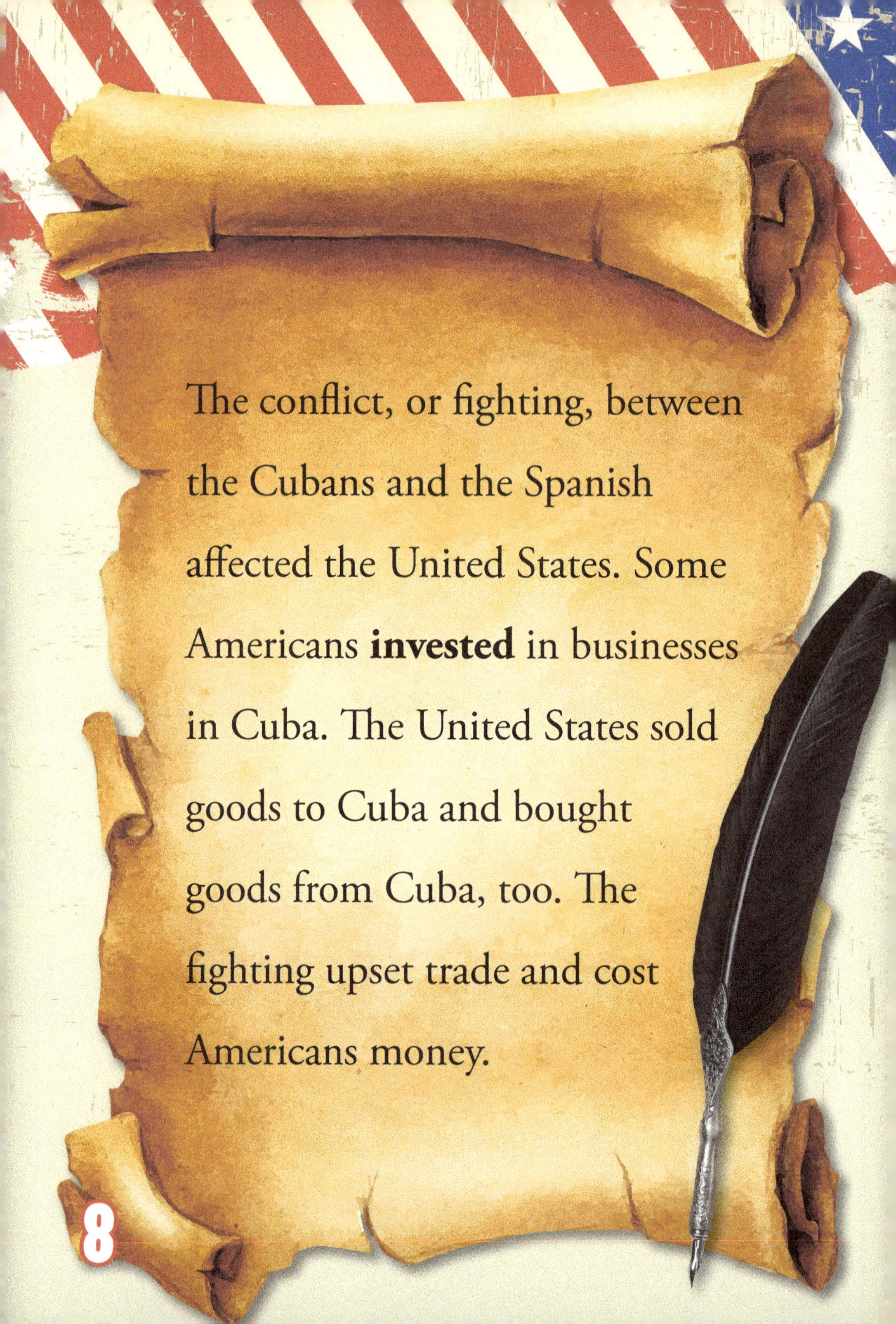

The conflict, or fighting, between the Cubans and the Spanish affected the United States. Some Americans **invested** in businesses in Cuba. The United States sold goods to Cuba and bought goods from Cuba, too. The fighting upset trade and cost Americans money.

MAKE THE GRADE

William McKinley (above) became US president in 1897. He wanted to stay out of the conflict in Cuba at first.

REMEMBER THE MAINE!

The warship called the USS *Maine* sailed to Cuba to help protect, or guard, Americans there. On February 15, 1898, an **explosion** sank the ship, killing more than 260 US sailors. The cause of the blast was unknown. Many Americans blamed Spain.

MAKE THE GRADE

In 1976, navy **investigators** reported that a fire appeared to have caused the explosion on the *Maine*. Spain likely had nothing to do with it.

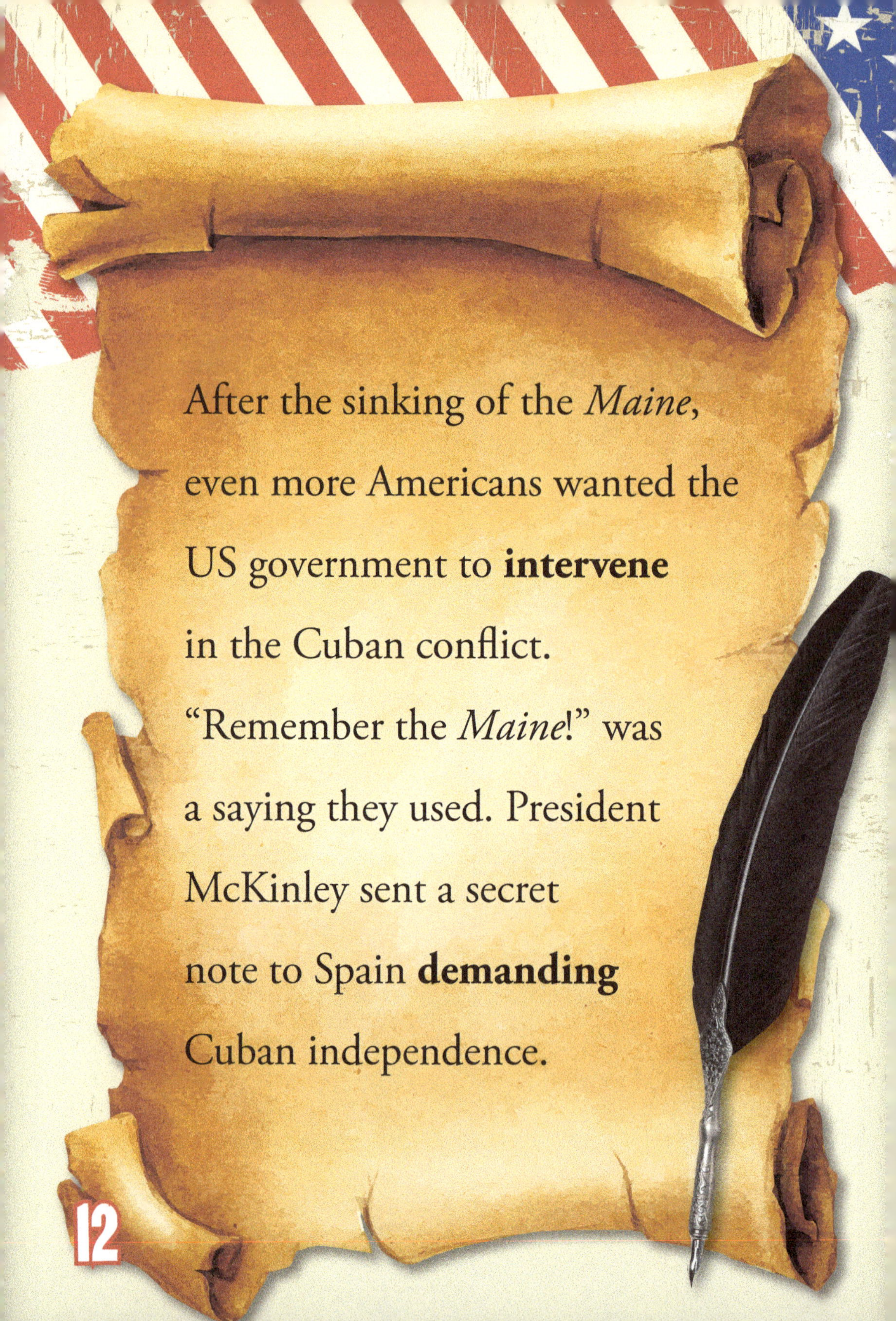

After the sinking of the *Maine*, even more Americans wanted the US government to **intervene** in the Cuban conflict. "Remember the *Maine*!" was a saying they used. President McKinley sent a secret note to Spain **demanding** Cuban independence.

MAKE THE GRADE

Spain tried to make peace with the Cuban rebels in 1897. However, by then, the Cubans wanted total independence.

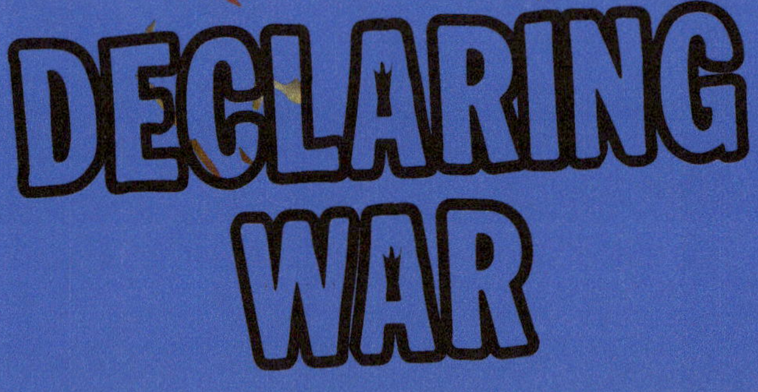

DECLARING WAR

On April 24, 1898, Spain **declared** war on the United States. The United States declared war on Spain the next day. The war was fought mostly in the Caribbean and in the Philippines. At the time, the Philippines was a Spanish colony in Southeast Asia.

MAKE THE GRADE

The United States promised not to seize, or take, Cuba as a US territory.

AMERICAN SOLDIERS HEAD TO THE SPANISH-AMERICAN WAR

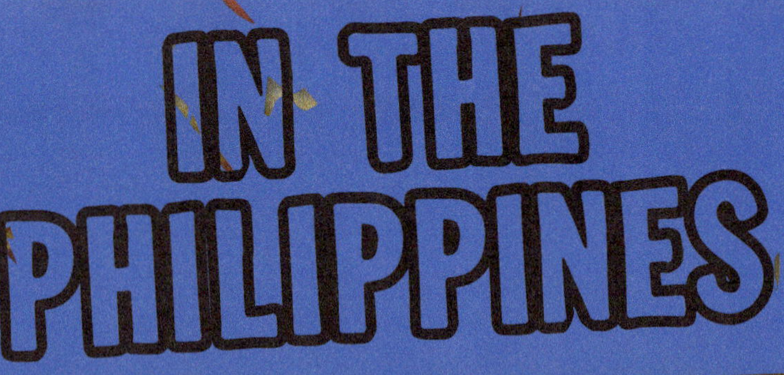

On May 1, 1898, **Commodore** George Dewey led the US Navy into Manila Bay in the Philippines. The US ships fired on the Spanish ships, destroying them. About 11,000 American soldiers arrived in the Philippines by the end of July 1898.

MAKE THE GRADE

American soldiers took control of the capital of the Philippines—Manila—by August 1898.

IN THE CARIBBEAN

The US Navy sent vessels, or ships, to Cuba, including four new warships. American ships stopped Spanish ships from leaving the harbor of the city of Santiago de Cuba. The US Army sent a force to fight on land, including many **volunteers**.

MAKE THE GRADE

The Rough Riders were a group of volunteer cavalry, or soldiers on horseback, with the US Army in Cuba. Future president Theodore Roosevelt was their leader.

THE BATTLE OF SAN JUAN HILL

The US Army headed toward Santiago de Cuba. The Spanish army had hilltop positions around the city. The Americans aimed to take these and gain control of the city. After heavy fighting, Americans won what was called the Battle of San Juan Hill.

MAKE THE GRADE

A group of African American soldiers stood out for their bravery during the Spanish-American War. They're sometimes called the Buffalo Soldiers.

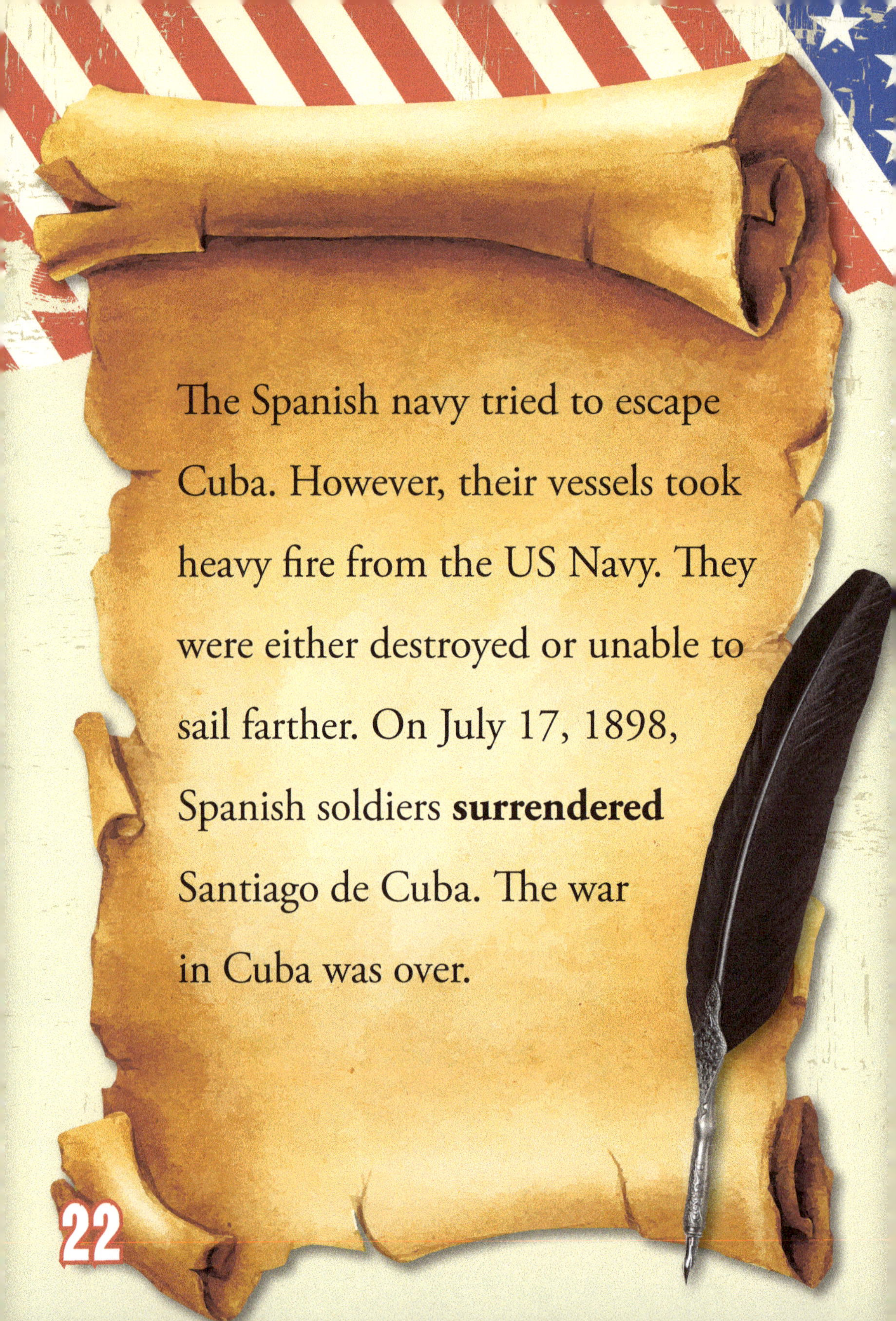

The Spanish navy tried to escape Cuba. However, their vessels took heavy fire from the US Navy. They were either destroyed or unable to sail farther. On July 17, 1898, Spanish soldiers **surrendered** Santiago de Cuba. The war in Cuba was over.

MAKE THE GRADE

In June 1898, the US Navy took control of the island of Guam, a Spanish territory in the western Pacific Ocean. The people there didn't even know there was a war!

THE TREATY OF PARIS

In October 1898, peace talks between Spain and the United States began in France. On December 10, the countries signed an agreement called the Treaty of Paris. Cuba received independence. Spain gave the United States its territories of Guam and Puerto Rico.

MAKE THE GRADE

The Spanish-American War was fought over about 10 weeks.

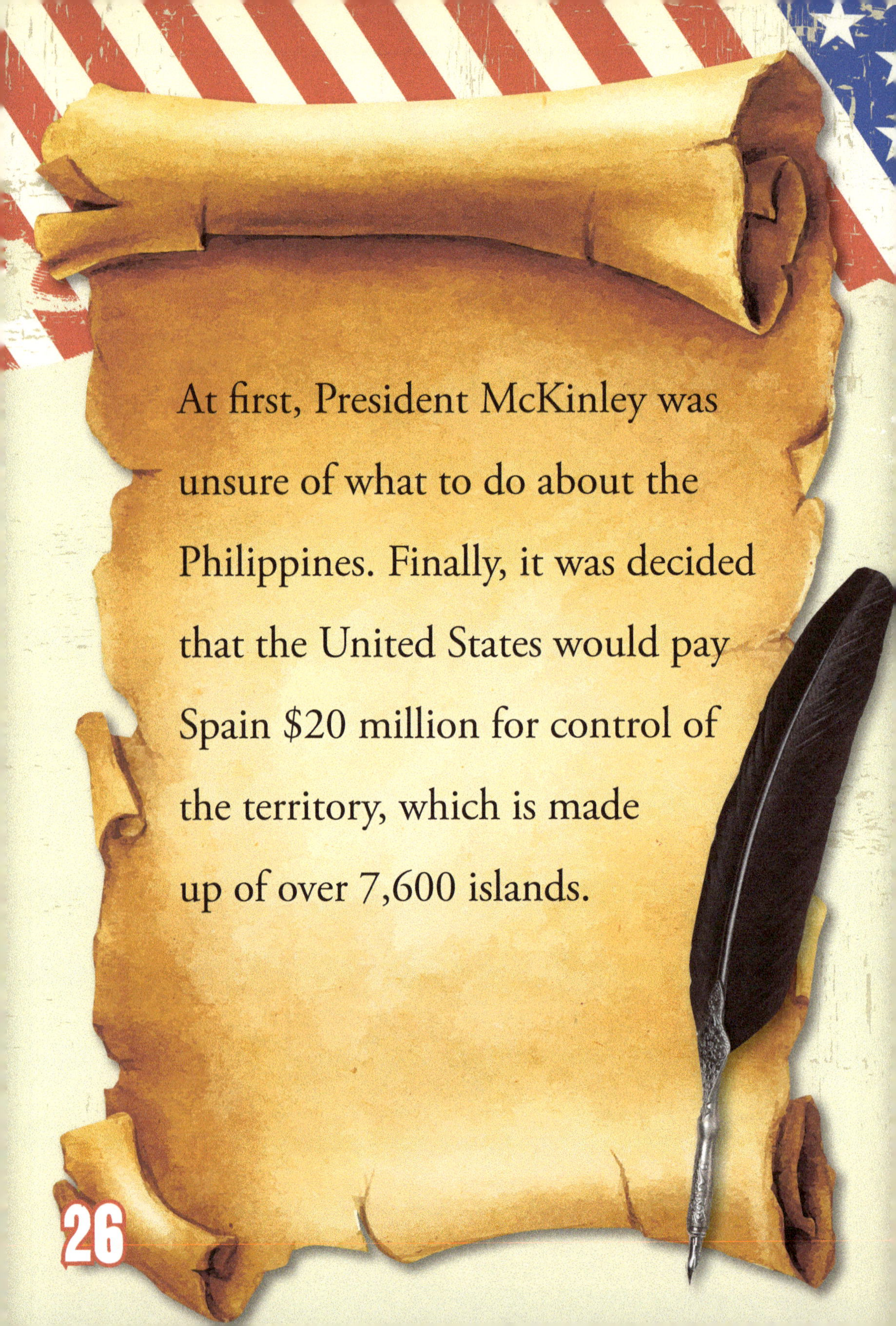

At first, President McKinley was unsure of what to do about the Philippines. Finally, it was decided that the United States would pay Spain $20 million for control of the territory, which is made up of over 7,600 islands.

MAKE THE GRADE

The people of the Philippines fought the United States for independence. They didn't gain independence until 1946.

AFTER THE WAR

Theodore Roosevelt was called a hero after the Spanish-American War. He became vice president in 1901. President McKinley was killed in September 1901. Roosevelt then became president of the United States, now a world power among nations.

MAKE THE GRADE

About 3,000 US soldiers died during the Spanish-American War. About 90 percent died of illnesses.

THEODORE ROOSEVELT

KEY DATES OF THE SPANISH-AMERICAN WAR

FEBRUARY 1895
Cuban rebels begin to fight against Spain.

FEBRUARY 15, 1898
An explosion sinks the USS *Maine*.

APRIL 24, 1898
Spain declares war on the United States.

APRIL 25, 1898
The United States declares war on Spain.

MAY 1, 1898
The US Navy defeats the Spanish in Manila Bay in the Philippines.

JULY 1, 1898
American forces win the Battle of San Juan Hill.

JULY 3, 1898
The US Navy defeats the Spanish navy near Cuba.

JULY 17, 1898
Spanish soldiers surrender Santiago de Cuba.

OCTOBER 1, 1898
Peace talks between Spain and the United States begin.

DECEMBER 10, 1898
Spain and the United States sign the Treaty of Paris.

GLOSSARY

colony: a piece of land under the control of another country

commodore: the name for a captain in the US Navy who commands more than one ship

declare: to say something officially

demand: to ask for something forcefully

explosion: a sudden release of energy

independence: the state of being free

intervene: to become a part of something to have an effect on the result

invest: to spend money on something in order to earn more money

investigator: one who searches for facts about something

rebel: one who fights to overthrow a government

surrender: to give up

territory: land controlled by a government

volunteer: a person who offers service without being asked

FOR MORE INFORMATION

Books

Baker, Brynn. *Roosevelt's Rough Riders: Fearless Cavalry of the Spanish-American War*. North Mankato, MN: Capstone Press, 2016.

Rice, Katelyn. *The Spanish-American War*. Huntington Beach, CA: Teacher Created Materials, Inc., 2017.

Websites

The Rough Riders Storm San Juan Hill, 1898
www.eyewitnesstohistory.com/roughriders.htm
Learn about this battle from those who were there.

The Spanish American War
www.ducksters.com/history/us_1800s/spanish-american_war.php
Read a short history of the war and learn some more facts.

Publisher's note to educators and parents: Our editors have carefully reviewed these websites to ensure that they are suitable for students. Many websites change frequently, however, and we cannot guarantee that a site's future contents will continue to meet our high standards of quality and educational value. Be advised that students should be closely supervised whenever they access the internet.

INDEX